THIS IS OUR SEDER

by **Ziporah Hildebrandt**
illustrated by **Robin Roraback**

Holiday House / New York

To anyone enjoying a Seder for the first time,
and to my daughter, Siviva, who inspired this book.

Text copyright © 1999 by Ziporah Hildebrandt
Illustrations copyright © 1999 by Robin Roraback
All Rights Reserved
Printed in the United States of America
First Edition
Library of Congress Cataloging-in-Publication Data
Hildebrandt, Ziporah, 1956–
This is our Seder / by Ziporah Hildebrandt; illustrated by Robin
Roraback.–1st ed.
p.   cm.
Summary: A simple description of the food and activities at a Seder, the
ritual meal of Passover, including an explanation of their historical and
symbolic significance.
ISBN 0-8234-1436-1 (reinforced)
1. Passover–Juvenile literature. 2. Seder–Juvenile literature. [l. Seder.
2. Passover. 3. Holidays.] I. Roraback, Robin, ill. II. Title.
BM695.P3H54 1999
296.4'5371–dc21   98-4194
CIP   AC

This is our night for coming together.

This is the plate for teaching,

the wine for blessing,

the water for washing,

the pillows for leaning,

the greens for dipping,

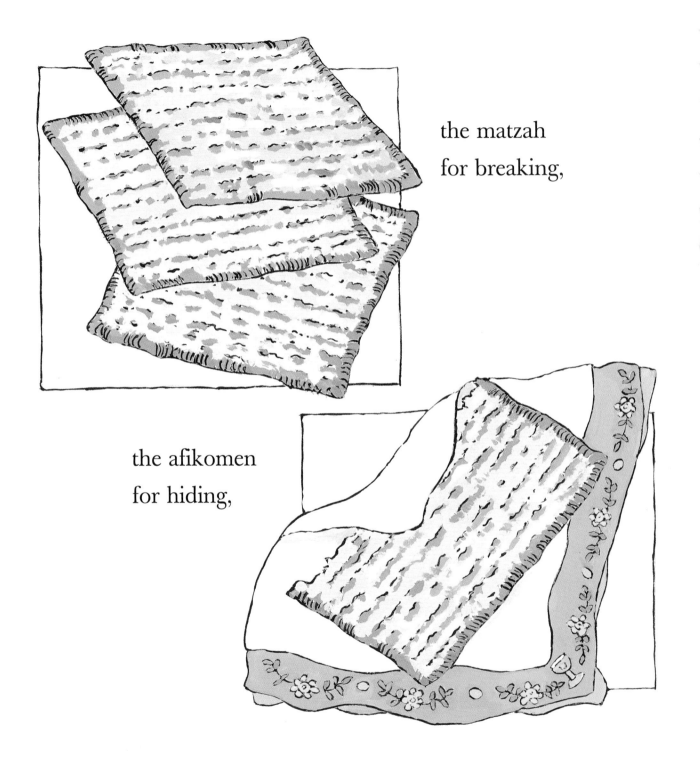

the matzah
for breaking,

the afikomen
for hiding,

the questions for asking,

the story for telling,

the horseradish for tasting,

the sandwich for making–

our yummy Seder meal
for gobbling up!

This is our thanks for all we've been given,
the songs of praise for lifting our hearts high.

This is the cup for Elijah.
We open the door . . .

This is our freedom!

The springtime holiday of Passover or Pesach (PAY-sock) commemorates the freedom of the Jewish people from slavery in Egypt. The story of this momentous time is incorporated into a ritual supper called a Seder (SAY-der).

There is a Seder on each of the first two nights of Passover. The Seder helps each person present understand the oppression of slavery and the blessings of freedom. Each person holds a Haggadah (ha-GA-da), a book describing the Seder ritual, which can take several hours to complete.

Particular foods symbolize elements of the Passover story during the Seder. Matzah (MAHTZ-a), unleavened bread, was the last bread baked in Egypt, with no time to rise before the people had to flee. Wine marks special moments of praise, blessing, or remembrance. Saltwater symbolizes the tears and bitterness of slavery.

The roasted egg, *betzah*, stands for the pilgrimage offering that was brought in later times to the Temple on certain holidays. The greens, *karpas*, symbolize spring, and can be any vegetable, even a potato. Horseradish is the bitter herb, *maror*, in remembrance of the bitterness of exile and bondage. *Charoset* (ha-RO-set) symbolizes the bricks and mortar the Israelites labored with under Pharaoh. Apples and nuts are the clay of the bricks, cinnamon stands for the straw, and the wine mixed in is for the blood spilled in slavery. The lamb bone on the Seder plate recalls the sacrificial lambs, whose blood on the Israelites' doorposts signaled the Angel of Death to "pass over" during the Tenth Plague.

Traditional preparations for the eight days of Passover are the most elaborate of the Jewish year. Every corner of the house is cleaned, and special food is eaten on dishes used only at this time. Passover is a time to remember and reflect, to seek meaning and to hope, to share and celebrate. The ritual of the Seder, rich in the meaning of thousands of years, can reveal deep insights into life, the present, and the past.